WATERSCAPE

水色 Waterscape
石井義人 Yoshito ISHII

作　品　集
編　　撰 / 張哲嘉 Tony Chang
藝　術　家 / 石井義人 Yoshito ISHII
編輯出版 / 宇達特文創有限公司
　　　　　台北市大安區敦化南路一段 312 號 (02)2700-6883
E - m a i l / service@urdct.com
視覺設計 / 優立方創意股份有限公司 (02)7750-7009
發　　行 / 時報文化出版企業股份有限公司
　　　　　台北市萬華區和平西路三段 240 號 (02)2306-6600
初版一刷 / 2023 年 11 月
定　　價 / 新台幣 800 元

ISBN　　　978-986-90070-5-4

目錄
Contents

Foreword
Paranoid perfectionist

Tony Chang
President of Taipei Culture and Creative International Association

The story of how I met Yoshihito Ishii is nothing short of a serendipitous twist of fate. In 2014, while attending a hotel art fair in Hong Kong, I stumbled upon Ishii's artworks. He had entrusted one of his pieces to be displayed at a gallery booth through an art intermediary. In the midst of the intricate hotel rooms, I laid eyes on Ishii's work for the first time. After a conversation with his representative, I decided to bring one of his pieces back to Taipei. This was actually the first artwork I collected at a hotel art fair, as I had previously purchased art by visiting galleries in Japan.

The artwork was a paper-based creation using meticulous drawing tools. Being a somewhat experienced art collector, I had often been reminded by senior collectors that the choice of artistic medium could affect future value. At that moment, I did contemplate letting it go, but the elegance and perfect presentation of the artwork, rather than its potential future value, struck me. What mattered was why he created it, not so much what he was doing.

Once I had the piece framed and brought it back to Taipei, it was prominently displayed in my gallery's office. It wasn't until the following summer, over a year later, that a stranger, an artist, paid a surprise visit to my gallery without any prior contact. He came across as sincere and a bit shy, clearly summoning a great deal of courage. I politely took his business card, not initially recognizing the artist behind the creation. Ishii did not speak Chinese and conversing in English wasn't easy, so I was contemplating a polite decline. However, I turned the card over and saw his work, which jogged my memory. I abruptly interrupted his nervous introduction, saying, "I have your artwork." The surprise must have caught him off guard. He widened his eyes in disbelief, as if he, too, believed it was a twist of fate. We then went to my office to see the artwork I had acquired in Hong Kong. I recall him standing in front of his artwork, seemingly stunned for about five seconds. It was clear he thought it was a sign from the universe.

He eventually gathered the courage to explain his purpose. In his notebook, he had listed the names and addresses of five galleries, saying, "I hope to find opportunities in Taiwan. I currently teach at a high school, and during this summer break, I planned to visit five galleries in Taipei. Uspace Gallery was his first stop, as he had heard in the Japanese art world that it specializes in contemporary Japanese artists. He said, 'I hope Uspace Gallery will represent me, and I won't need to visit the other four galleries.'" Without hesitation, I agreed, and thus began our journey as partners in the art market.

For an artist like Yoshihito Ishii in the realm of contemporary art, his willingness to use meticulous precision as the foundation for abstract creations is quite rare. This is especially remarkable in a society dominated by speed and cost-effectiveness. He adds an element of unwavering commitment akin to ancient scholars' pursuit of excellence. Whether he is a visionary genius or a Don Quixote bravely facing challenges, his work consistently defies expectations.

Marcel Duchamp introduced numerous concepts in the early 20th century that influenced the definition of contemporary art for subsequent generations. Using these concepts to define the "value" of Ishii's work is quite apt. Apart from the aesthetic influence of Song Dynasty literati painting, he seeks to challenge whether abstract art should be "casual" and how his logical approach leads to error-free creations. He has transitioned from using a 0.2mm pen to 0.1mm, from slightly bolder structures to increasingly intricate compositions, and from 1F-sized artworks to 10F-sized ones, even reaching the current largest size of 130F. He flawlessly presents each artwork without any revisions. In reality, such medium and composition cannot be corrected. I once spent a day carefully examining the details of his work, and even those new to art could easily discern the logical elements in his pieces.

His creations are less "meticulous" and more akin to "precise," akin to a semiconductor wafer. In my nearly 20 years of interacting with Japanese artists, few can create such soft imagery with such unwavering dedication and hard work, carving out a different path in abstract art. Friends with painting experience would know that this requires a keen eye and steady hands. He truly pours his life into his creations, and thus, his limited annual output makes his work rare and sought-after. Seeing his works beyond size 20 is extremely rare, and collecting works beyond size 30 is truly a matter of serendipity.

Having represented Ishii for nearly a decade, I've noticed that many people who see his work for the first time often find it difficult to distinguish between pieces. However, experienced collectors can easily recognize the differences in his work and even determine whether they are from the same period. I believe his work continues to challenge limits and evolve.

偏執的完美

張哲嘉

台北文化創意協會 理事長

說起與石井義人認識的故事，只能說是上天巧妙的安排…

2014 年我在香港的飯店博覽會中發現石井的作品，當時他委託一個藝術 intermediary 在某家參展畫廊的展間，在繁復的飯店房間內，我第一眼就看到石井的作品，與他當時的代理人交談後，我就帶了他一幅作品回到台北了。其實這件作品是我第一件在飯店博覽會收藏的作品，在以前我都是參訪日本畫廊購買作品的。這是一幅使用繪圖器材的紙上作品，對於有小有收藏經驗的我來說，收藏家前輩時常提醒，創作媒材的不同會影響未來的價格。也因此當下確實有閃過放棄的念頭，但是看到作品本身的優雅線條與呈現出來的完美形象，那個所謂"收藏未來的價格"好像也沒那麼重要了，重點是他為什麼做，而不是在意他在做什麼。

這件作品帶回台北裱框後，一直掛在我的畫廊辦公室。直到隔年的暑假，有位陌生藝術家沒有聯繫就直接來畫廊拜訪，給我的第一印象是誠懇又羞澀，看得出他提起了極大的勇氣，生澀的介紹自己。我禮貌地接過名片，其實事隔一年多我也忘記那件作品的創作著是誰，石井他不會說中文也不容易用英文交談，原本想要禮貌地拒絕當下，我看了名片的背面印著他的作品，我忽然打斷了他生澀的對話，我說：「我有你的作品。」應該是

被突如其來的巧合驚嚇吧？這人當下將他瞇瞇的眼睛瞪得像龍眼一樣大，說話說完隨即帶他到我的辦公室看當時在香港買的作品。記得他當下驚呆了站在他作品前面，應該停頓了有五秒，應該是他也認為是上天的安排吧？

後來他終於鼓起勇氣說明來意，攤開的筆記本中記著五家畫廊的名字與地址說著：「我希望能夠在台灣尋找發展，目前在高中任教，趁這次暑假的時間計劃來台北拜訪五家畫廊，而 Uspace Gallery 是他此行的第一站，因為在日本業界就聽說這是海外專門經營日本當代藝術家的畫廊。」石井如此對我說著我：「希望 Uspace Gallery 能夠經紀我，而不會想要再拜訪其他四家畫廊了。」當下我也不假思索地答應了，因而開啓了我們與石井義人在藝術市場並肩而戰的故事。

以石井義人這樣的當代藝術家來說，願意以工筆偏執的能量來做為抽象創作的基底，是極為少見的，尤其在這充滿快速與信價比的社會氛圍來說，他多了一份像古人擇善固執的精神。若他不是一位有遠見的天才，那就是一位努力面對惡龍的唐吉軻德。

杜象 (Marcel Duchamp) 在 20 世紀初所提出許多的概念，他影響了後世的當代藝術的定義。

而用這些概念來定義石井義人作品的"價值"

總是非常恰當的，除宋朝院體派對他創作的美學影響外，他想挑戰的是抽象創作是否應該"隨性"以及自己如此完美邏輯之下所創作的作品如何會出錯？從原本 0.2mm 的針筆到 0.1mm、稍粗曠的結構到越發細緻的構圖、1F 的作品到 10F 的作品，甚至到目前最大的 130F，他都能對作品毫無修補的完美呈現。實際上這樣的媒材與構圖是無法修補的，我曾經花了一天的時間仔細觀察作品中的各項細節，就算是剛開始接觸藝術的朋友，都能輕易看出作品元素的邏輯。

這樣的作品與其說"工筆"，不如說是像台積電晶圓 (Wafer) 一樣的"精確"、"完美"，我近 20 年來接觸了不少日本藝術家經驗，極少人能以這樣極盡偏執的硬底子功夫，創造出如此柔軟的意象，自成一格的走出抽象創作一條不同的路。有學過畫的朋友就會知道，這需要十足的眼力、手勁，只能說他真的是以生命在創作，所以他作品每年的產量十分有限與稀有，能夠看到他超過 20 號的作品非常不容易，能夠收藏到超過 30 號的作品真的要看造化了。

經紀石井近十年的經驗來說，許多第一次看他作品的人都覺得作品很像，不好分辨。但是有經驗的藏家非常容易就能分辨他作品的不同，甚至是否為同時期的作品，我認為他作品到現在還在挑戰極限並演化中。

Fractal Wonders of Superimposed Ukiyo-e

Kai-Huang CHEN
Interdisciplinary Conceptual Artist
President of Taipei Naitonal University of the Arts

Yoshito Ishii's artistic creations are a direct reflection of the contemporary life vocabulary and inner joy of the present era, drawing deeply from Japan's cross-century heritage. Several layers of aes-thetics reveal the sincerity within:

Rooted in a transcultural Asian context, Ishii's works serve as a medium of artistic expression and a conduit for historical, intangible consciousness. They are both pure and serene, evoking a quiet resonance that is easily overlooked.

The forms and shapes in his art traverse from the microcosmic to the macrocosmic, and even when challenging our perceptions, they retain their inherent meaning and value. The snowflake-like formations are not confined to human perspectives but rather represent a transition of reality into abstract thought, extending infinitely from reality to fractal expansion.
The amalgamation of unreal colors transcends dualities, bridging the gap between opposites like positive and negative, past and present, large and small, real and abstract, cold and hot, and more.

This simplicity resonates with poetic worlds, moving from poetics to becoming the precursor of po-etics, offering a minimalist sense of happiness.

The dynamic nature of the artistic medium and its forms is not confined to a single canvas. The boundaries of his works shift in harmony with the world's every breath, adopting shapes ranging from squares to circles and more.

This creative process epitomizes the replacement of spatial entities by temporal processes, ex-panding individual evolution from the visual to the realm of perception. It signifies a contemporary, tranquil artistic endeavor, a personalized journey shared by the artist with everyone. It encom-passes silent joy, inner contentment, and how we view ourselves and others when taking each breath—a gift of empathy and sharing, a return to the essence of life.

We understand that this process can be lavish and magnificent, but it can also be an apt embodi-ment, much like the philosophy of life.

超昇浮世繪的碎形萬象

陳愷璜

跨領域觀念藝術家
國立臺北藝術大學 校長

石井義人的繪畫性創作，無華中汲飲著日本的跨世紀傳承，直白地透露著屬於當下時代的生活語彙及其內在歡愉。從幾個具體層次的美學體現，便不難察覺如此的真摯特性：

從修為而來的跨亞洲文化意涵，轉介作為表現的技術媒介，硬筆輪廓線是繼往開來的一套歷史的無形意識也已經是文化的集體潛意識，既淳淨也安靜，卻容易令人錯失它質純的汩汩聲響。

形式與形態上都是從微觀到巨觀的體現，甚至是認知的反轉也仍然不失其實存的意義與價值：雪花般的造型，不是人的眼界，而是現實進入抽象思維轉化的情境。從實境到碎形的無限擴充與蔓延。

它的非現實色彩總成，跨越正反、前後、大小、虛實、冷熱 ... 等兩極的單純辨證；只奉獻給詩化的世界，從詩性（poétique）到成為詩性（poiétique）的前趨，這得以成為極簡的幸福感受！

載體型態（造型）與種類的流動式承載：除了不固定在單一的載體選用外，作品的邊界也跟著外部世界的每一次呼吸而隨時滑移而獲得安置。方形、圓形、... 不一而足！

因此，這樣的創作型態，完整體現著時間過程替代空間實體的有限性，擴增著從視覺到感知體悟的個體進化，成為一種當代沈靜的藝術企圖。這是藝術家足以與每一個人分享的個體化過程：無聲歡愉、沈靜裡的寬慰、如何看待呼吸時候的自己與他人：一種同理心與分享的禮物、回返生活自身。

我們都知道，這種過程可以很絢爛，非常華麗；但是，也可能就只是給出一種恰如其分的實存，一如生命哲學。

石井 義人
Yoshito ISHII

1980 年　群馬県伊勢崎市生まれ　高崎市在住
2003 年　日本大学芸術学部美術学科絵画コース版画専攻卒業

受賞歴
1999 年　群馬青年ビエンナーレ '99　入選
2010 年　第 26 回 FUKUI サムホール美術展　入選
　　　　　第 6 回全国公募西脇市サムホール美術展　入選
2012 年　第 17 回アートムーブ絵画コンクール　ドリーム賞
　　　　　第 29 回 FUKUI サムホール美術展　入選
　　　　　第 7 回西脇市サムホール美術展　入選
2014 年　大細密展　優秀賞
　　　　　第 9 回全国公募西脇市サムホール美術展　入選
　　　　　第 31 回 FUKUI サムホール美術展　奨励賞
2015 年　第 8 回清須絵画トリエンナーレ　佳作
2016 年　第 33 回 FUKUI サムホール美術展　入選
2017 年　第 34 回 FUKUI サムホール美術展　入選
2020 年　第 37 回 FUKUI サムホール美術展　入選

個展
2009 年　イシイヨシト「阿吽」SAKuRA GALLERY 東京
2011 年　イシイヨシト・ペン画展「ani-millimism」FUMA CONTEMPORARY TOKYO
2014 年　イシイヨシト・ペン画展「線乃ざわめき。」The Art complex Center of Tokyo
2015 年　イシイヨシト・ペン画展「続・線乃ざわめき。」ギャルリー志門
2016 年　渺渺 – 極線之美　Uspace Gallery 台北
2017 年　一線入魂　Uspace Gallery 台北
2018 年　繾綣 Touching　Uspace Gallery 台北
2020 年　熾 Flourishing　Uspace Gallery 台北
2021 年　水色 WATERSCAPE　Uspace Gallery 台北
2022 年　水色 vol.2 WATERSCAPE　Uspace Gallery 台北

グループ展
1999 年　群馬青年ビエンナーレ '99　群馬県立近代美術館　群馬
2000 年　デザインフェスタ vol.11 東京ビッグサイト　東京
2002 年　第 26 回全国大学版画展　国際版画美術館　東京
2003 年　東京五美術大学連合卒業・修了制作展　東京都美術館　東京
2010 年　N + N 展 2010　春の嵐：日藝美術出身の若手作家達の今　練馬区立
　　　　　美術館　東京
　　　　　meet 展　SAKuRA GALLERY 東京
　　　　　第 26 回 FUKUI サムホール美術展　福井カルチャーセンター　福井
　　　　　第 6 回全国公募西脇市サムホール美術展　西脇岡之山美術館　兵庫
　　　　　デザインフェスタ vol.32 東京ビッグサイト　東京
　　　　　芸法大賞　兵庫県立美術館、兵庫
2011 年　ACT アート大賞展　The Art complex Center of Tokyo 東京
　　　　　細密展 2011　The Art complex Center of Tokyo 東京
　　　　　N + N 展 2011　生命を見つめる　練馬区立美術館　東京
　　　　　全国サムホール公募展　交通会館　東京
　　　　　あおぞら DE アート 8 人展　SAKuRA gallery　東京
　　　　　あおぞら DE アート　泰明小学校　東京
　　　　　細密展 3　The Art complex Center of Tokyo 東京
　　　　　クリスマスにギャラリーエデルへサンタがプレゼントを持ってき展
　　　　　ギャラリーエデル　京都
2012 年　MOVIE 展　バー JOINT　神奈川
　　　　　細密展 4　The Art complex Center of Tokyo 東京
　　　　　第 17 回アートムーブ絵画コンクール展 大阪
　　　　　第 29 回 FUKUI サムホール美術展　福井カルチャーセンター　福井
　　　　　大細密展　The Art complex Center of Tokyo 東京
　　　　　CHIPS2012　代官山ヒルサイドテラス　東京
　　　　　第 7 回西脇市サムホール美術展　西脇市岡之山美術館　兵庫
　　　　　巡回展 The Art complex Center of Tokyo 東京、同時代ギャラリー　京都
　　　　　デザインフェスタ vol.36　東京ビッグサイト　東京
2013 年　Sensai 展 The Art complex Center of Tokyo 東京
　　　　　デザインフェスタ vol.37　東京ビッグサイト　東京
　　　　　大細密展 2013 The Art complex Center of Tokyo 東京
　　　　　常設展 gallery art soup　群馬

裏カーボンブラック　SELF-SO gallery　京都
L'ART CONTEMPORAIN JAPONAIS,UNE IDENTITÉ PARTICULIÈRE　フランス
Art Wave Exhibition- 創造のイノベーション - RECTO VERSO GALLERY　東京
デザインフェスタ vol.38　東京ビッグサイト　東京
COLORS TO GO 日本藝術家 25 人 BATTLE 展　25TOGO BRIGHT　高雄
2014 年　ACT 小品展 2014　The Art complex Center of Tokyo　東京
　　　　C/LABORATORY PROJECT@ Hong Kong Contemporary 2014　香港
　　　　大細密展 2014　The Art complex Center of Tokyo　東京
　　　　第 31 回 FUKUI サムホール美術展　福井カルチャーセンター　福井
　　　　ACT+ISM　The Art complex Center of Tokyo　東京
　　　　C/LABORATORY PROJECT@ Asia Contemporary Art Show 2014　香港
　　　　アートの贈り物 - 眠れない夜に - 　銀座三越　東京
2015 年　細密展 2015　The Art complex Center of Tokyo　東京
　　　　清須市第 8 回はるひ絵画トリエンナーレ　清須市はるひ美術館　愛知
　　　　大細密展 2015　The Art complex Center of Tokyo　東京
　　　　ART CASE -My Digital Life 25TOGO BRIGHT　高雄
2016 年　語る抽象画展　The Art complex Center of Tokyo　東京
　　　　Infinity Japan 2016 Contemporary Art Show in Taipei　台北
　　　　小名木川バラッド　SAKuRA Gallery　東京
　　　　細密展 2016　The Art complex Center of Tokyo　東京
　　　　デザインフェスタ vol.43　東京ビッグサイト　東京
　　　　第 33 回 FUKUI サムホール美術展　福井カルチャーセンター　福井
　　　　大細密展 2016　The Art complex Center of Tokyo　東京
　　　　神戸アートマルシェ 2016　兵庫
　　　　METRO ART vol.25 @ 東京サンケイビル秋まつり　東京
　　　　細密展 9　The Art complex Center of Tokyo　東京
2017 年　METRO ART vol.26 東京サンケイビル　東京
　　　　Infinity Japan 2017 Contemporary Art Show in Taipei　台北
　　　　細密展 11　The Art complex Center of Tokyo　東京
　　　　アートスープ・クロニクル　gallery art soup　群馬
　　　　Cross the River　SAKuRA Gallery　東京
　　　　大細密展 2017　The Art complex Center of Tokyo　東京
　　　　水無月 - 日本當代藝術特展　Uspace Gallery　台北　台湾
　　　　第 34 回 FUKUI サムホール美術展　福井カルチャーセンター　福井
　　　　アートフェアアジア福岡　ホテルオークラ福岡　福岡
　　　　神戸アートマルシェ 2017　兵庫
　　　　高秋山景　SAKuRA Gallery　東京
ペン画三人展　創世の細部　ギャラリーボイス　岩手
2018 年　Infinity Japan 2018・プレエキシビション　Uspace Gallery　台北
　　　　細密展 12 - 緻 -　The Art complex Center of Tokyo　東京

Infinity Japan 2018 Contemporary Art Show in Taipei　台北
Artsoup in Colmena vol.2　Colmena Gallery & Art Space　沖縄
アートフェア東京 2018　東京国際フォーラム　東京
アートフェア東京 2018 期間内展示　石川画廊　東京
EXTRA ART 2　The Art complex Center of Tokyo　東京
小収蔵紀念日　Uspace Gallery 台北　台湾
PIA 展　ギャラリー・オーツー　群馬
アートフェアアジア福岡 2018　ホテルオークラ福岡　福岡
神戸アートマルシェ 2018　兵庫
柴田貴史　豊澤めぐみ　イシイヨシト展　SAKuRA Gallery　東京
2019 年　細密画展　CLOUDS ART+COFFEE　東京
　　　　細密展 14　The Art complex Center of Tokyo　東京
　　　　線の迷宮　Uspace Gallery　台北　台湾
　　　　Infinity Japan 2019 Contemporary Art Show in Taipei　台北
　　　　アートフェアアジア福岡 2019　ホテルオークラ福岡　福岡
　　　　神戸アートマルシェ 2019　兵庫
　　　　SMALL WONDERS ART SHOW 2019 - 2020　CLOUD ART+COFFEE　東京
2020 年　第 2 回アートセレクション展　ギャラリー・オーツー　群馬
　　　　遊春《spring fun》　豊藝館　台中
　　　　KaNAM Art Wall COLORS 展　軽井沢ニューアートミュージアム　長野
　　　　大細密展 2020　The Art complex Center of Tokyo　東京
　　　　難以想像 - 極 細密展　Uspace Gallery　台北　台湾
　　　　イシイヨシト　白鳥雅也　二人展　SAKuRA Gallery　東京
　　　　第 37 回 FUKUI サムホール美術展 in 金津創作の森　福井
　　　　細密展 16　The Art complex Center of Tokyo　東京
　　　　Infinity Japan 2020　Uspace Gallery　台北
2021 年　青に秘める展その二　The Art complex Center of Tokyo　東京
　　　　PIA 展　ギャラリー・オーツー　群馬
　　　　春的符碼學 Hidden code in the Spring 畫展　Uspace Gallery　台北
　　　　大細密展 2021　The Art complex Center of Tokyo　東京
　　　　アートプロジェクト高崎 2021　高崎駅周辺　群馬
2022 年　新春小品展 2022　The Art complex Center of Tokyo　東京
　　　　墨色極光　Uspace Gallery　台北　台湾
　　　　青に秘める展 3　The Art complex Center of Tokyo　東京
　　　　PIA 展 2022　ギャラリー・オーツー　群馬
　　　　Infinity Japan 2022　Uspace Gallery　台北
2023 年　常設展 -《癸卯 8》Uspace Gallery　台北
　　　　イシイヨシト シガハルカ 2 人展　SAKuRA Gallery　東京
　　　　PIA 展　ギャラリー・オーツー　群馬
Infinity Japan 2023 Contemporary Art Show in Taipei　台北

Yoshito ISHII

1980   Born in Isesaki City,Gunma,Japan ,Living in Takasaki City,Gunma,Japan
2002   Graduated from Nihon University College Of Art, The Department Of Fine Arts, Tokyo, Japan

Awards

1999   Selected for Biennale of Young Artist Gunma
2010   Selected for The 27th Competition of Fukui Thumbhole Size Painting
        Selected for The 8th Competition of Nishiwaki Thumbhole Size Painting
2012   Selected for The 9th Competition of Nishiwaki Thumbhole Size Painting
        Selected for The 29th Competition of Fukui Thumbhole Size Painting
        Dream Award for The 17th Art Move Award
        Award of Excellence for DaiSaimitsu Exhibition
2014   Encouragement Award for The 31th Competition of Fukui Thumbhole Size Painting
2015   A fine work for The 8th Kiyosu City Painting triennale
2016   Selected for The 33th Competition of Fukui Thumbhole Size Painting
2017   Selected for The 34th Competition of Fukui Thumbhole Size Painting
2020   Selected for The 37th Competition of Fukui Thumbhole Size Painting

Solo Exhibitions

2009 A-Un(阿吽),at Sakura Gallery,Tokyo,Japan
2011 Ani-Millimism, at FUMA CONTEMPORARY Tokyo/BUNKYO ART,Tokyo,Japan
2014 Sen no Zawameki(線乃ざわめき), at The Art Complex Center of Tokyo,Tokyo,Japan
2015 Zoku Sen no Zawameki(続・線乃ざわめき), at Gallery Shimon,Tokyo,Japan
2016   ByoByo -Kyokusen no bi-(渺渺 - 極線の美 -)at Uspace gallery,Taipei,Taiwan
2017 Issen Nyukon(一線入魂), at Uspace gallery,Taipei,Taiwan
2018   Touching(繾綣),at Uspace Gallery,Taipei,Taiwan
2020 熾 Flourishing, at Uspace Gallery,Taipei,Taiwan
2021   水色 WATERSCAPE, at Uspace Gallery,Taipei,Taiwan
2022   水色 vol.2 WATERSCAPE, at Uspace Gallery,Taipei,Taiwan

Group Exhibitions

1999   Gunma Biennale for Young Artists 99', Museum of Modern Art Gunma,Gunma
2000   Design Festa Vol.11, Tokyo Big Sight,Tokyo
2002   The 26th Annual Exhibition of The Association of Japanese Art Colleges, Tokyo
2003   Joint Graduation Exhibition of Five Art Universities in Tokyo, Tokyo
        Meets, at Sakura Gallery,Tokyo
        The 26th Fukui Thumb Hole Art Exhibition, Fukui Culture Center, Fukui
        The 8th Okanoyama Museum of Art Nishiwaki Thumbhole Art Exhibition Award
        Design Festa vol.32, Tokyo Big Sight, Tokyo
        Geiho Exhibition, Hyogo Prefectural Art Museum, Hyogo
2011   ACT Art Award, The Art Complex Center of Tokyo,Tokyo
        The 3rd Saimitsu Exhibition 2011, The Art Complex Center of Tokyo
        Aozora De Art Exhibition, Sakura Gallery,Tokyo
        Aozora De Art, Taimei Primary School, Tokyo
        Santa Claus Is Coming To Gallery Edel at Christmas, Gallery Edel, Kyoto
2012   The 4th Saimitsu Exhibition, The Art Complex Center of Tokyo
        MOVIE Exhibition, BAR Joint, Kanagawa
        The 7th Okanoyama Museum of Art Nishiwaki Thumbhole Art Exhibition Award
        The 17th Art Move Award, Osaka
        DaiSaimitsu Exhibition, The Art Complex Center of Tokyo
        The 29th Fukui Thumbhole Art Exhibition, Fukui Culture Center, Fukui
        CHIPS 2012, Daikanyama Hillside Terrace, Tokyo
        Design Festa vol.36, Tokyo Big Sight,Tokyo
        Junkai Exhibition, The Art Complex Center of Tokyo, Tokyo
2013   Sensai Exhibition, The Art Complex Center of Tokyo,Tokyo
        Design Festa vol.37, Tokyo Big Sight,Tokyo
        DaiSaimitsu Exhibition 2013, The Art Complex Center of Tokyo
        Permanent Exhibition, Gallery Art Soup,Gunma
        Ura Carbon Black, SELF-SO gallery, Kyoto
        L'art contemporain JAPONAIS, , Galerie Robespierre, France
        Art Wave Exhibition, RECTO VERSO GALLERY, Tokyo
        Design Festa vol.38, Tokyo Big Sight,Tokyo
        COLORS TO GO, at 25TOGO BRIGHT, Kaohsiung

2014　Shohin Exhibition2014,at The Art Complex Center of Tokyo, Tokyo
　　　C/LABORATORY PROJECT@ HONG KONG CONTEMPORARY 2014, Hong Kong
　　　DaiSaimitsu Exbihition2014, The Art Complex Center of Tokyo
　　　The 31th Fukui Thumbhole Art Exhibition, Fukui Culture Center, Fukui
　　　ACT+ISM, The Art complex Center of Tokyo, Tokyo
　　　C/LABORATORY PROJECT@ Asia Contemporary Art Show 2014, Hong Kong
　　　Gift Of Art -For Sleepless Night- at Ginza Mitsukoshi,Tokyo
2015　Saimitsu Exbihition 2015, The Art Complex Center of Tokyo
　　　The 8th Kiyosu City Haruhi Painting Triennale,at Kiyosu Haruhi Museum, Aichi
　　　DaiSaimitsu Exhibition 2015, The Art Complex Center of Tokyo
　　　ART CASE –My Digital Life-, 25 TO GO BRIGHT, Kaohsiung
2016　Talking Abstract Paintings Exhibition, The Art Complex Center of Tokyo
　　　Infinity Japan 2016 Contemporary Art Show, MIRAMAR GARDEN TAIPEI, Taipei
　　　Onagigawa Ballad, SAKuRA Gallery,Tokyo
　　　Saimitsu Exhibition 2016, The Art Complex Center of Tokyo
　　　Design Festa vol.43, Tokyo Big Sight,Tokyo
　　　The 33th Fukui Thumbhole Art Exhibition, Fukui Culture Center, Fukui
　　　DaiSaimitsu Exhibition 2016, The Art Complex Center of Tokyo, Tokyo
　　　Kobe Art Marche, Kobe Meriken Park Hotel, Hyogo
　　　METRO ART vol.25 @Tokyo Sankei building Autumn Festival, Japan
　　　Saimitsu Exhibition 9, The Art Complex Center of Tokyo
2017　METRO ART vol.26, Tokyo Sankei building
　　　Infinity Japan 2017 Contemporary Art Show, MIRAMAR GARDEN TAIPEI, Taipei
　　　Saimitsu Exhibition 11, The Art Complex Center of Tokyo
　　　Art Soup chronicle, Gallery Art Soup, Gunma
　　　Cross the River, SAKuRA Gallery,Tokyo
　　　DaiSaimitsu Exhibition 2017, The Art Complex Center of Tokyo
　　　Minaduki-Japanese Contemporary Art Special Exhibition, Uspace gallery,Taipei
　　　The 34th Fukui Thumbhole Art Exhibition, Fukui Culture Center, Fukui
　　　Art Fair Asia Fukuoka, Hotel Okura Fukuoka,Fukuoka
　　　Kobe Art Marche 2017, Kobe Meriken Park Hotel, Hyogo
　　　Kosyu sankei, SAKuRA Gallery, Tokyo
　　　Detail of Genesis, Gallery Voice,Iwate
2018　Infinity Japan 2018 Pre-Exhibition, Uspace Gallery,Taipei
　　　Saimitsu Exhibition 12, The Art Complex Center of Tokyo
　　　Infinity Japan 2018 Contemporary Art Show, Hotel Royal Nikko Taipei
　　　Artsoup in Colmena vol.2, Colmena Gallery & Art Space,Okinawa

　　　ART FAIR TOKYO 2018, Tokyo International Forum, Tokyo
　　　Permanent Exhibition(during ART FAIR TOKYO 2018), Ishikawa Gallery, Tokyo
　　　EXTRA ART 2, The Art complex Center of Tokyo
　　　Small art Collection Memorial, Uspace Gallery,Taipei
　　　PIA Exhibition, Gallery O-TWO,Gunma
　　　Art Fair Asia Fukuoka 2018, Hotel Okura Fukuoka,Fukuoka
　　　Kobe Art Marche2018, Kobe Meriken Park Hotel, Hyogo
　　　Takashi Shibata Megumi Toyosawa Yoshito Ishii Exhibition, SAKuRA Gallery, Tokyo
2019　Saimitsuga Exhibition, CLOUDS ART+ COFFEE,Tokyo
　　　Saimitsu Exhibition 14, The Art Complex Center of Tokyo,Tokyo
　　　Psychedelic Line, Uspace Gallery, Taipei
　　　Infinity Japan 2019 Contemporary Art Show, Hotel Royal Nikko Taipei
　　　Art Fair Asia Fukuoka 2019, Hotel Okura Fukuoka,Fukuoka
　　　Kobe Art Marche 2019, Kobe Meriken Park Hotel, Hyogo
　　　SMALL WONDERS ART SHOW 2019 - 2020, CLOUD ART+COFFEE,Tokyo
2020　The 2nd Art Selection Exhibition, Gallery O-TWO,Gunma
　　　Spring Fun, Fong-Yi Art Gallery, Taichung
　　　DaiSaimitsu Exhibition 2020, The Art Complex Center of Tokyo
　　　KaNAM Art Wall COLORS Exhibition, Karuizawa New Art Museum,Nagano
　　　Unbelievable-Ultramicroscopic Exhibition, Uspace Gallery,Taipei
　　　Yoshito Ishii, Masaya Shiratori Duel Exhibition, SAKuRA Gallery,Tokyo
　　　The 37th Fukui Thumbhole Art Exhibition in Kanazu Forest of Creation, Fukui
　　　Saimitsu Exhibition 16, The Art Complex Center of Tokyo
　　　Infinity Japan 2020 Special Exhibition, Uspace Gallery,Taipei
2021　Keep It Blue Exhibition Part2, The Art Complex Center of Tokyo
　　　PIA Exhibition, Gallery O-TWO, Gunma
　　　Hidden code in the Spring, Uspace Gallery Taipei
　　　DaiSaimitsu Exhibition 2021, The Art Complex Center of Tokyo
　　　Art Project Takasaki, Around Takasaki station, Gunma
2022　ACT 15th Anniversary Exhibition, The Art Complex Center of Tokyo
　　　BLACK AURORA, Uspace Gallery Taipei
　　　Keep It Blue Exhibition Part2, The Art Complex Center of Tokyo
　　　PIA Exhibition, Gallery O-TWO, Gunma
　　　Infinity Japan 2022 Special Exhibition, Uspace Gallery, Taipei
2023　Guimao8, Uspace Gallery, Taipei
　　　Yoshito Ishii, Haruka Shiga Duel Exhibition, SAKuRA Gallery,Tokyo
　　　PIA Exhibition, Gallery O-TWO, Gunma
　　　Infinity Japan 2023 Contemporary Art Show, Hotel Royal Nikko Taipei

Concept
創作理念

色彩について

二冊目の作品集の刊行に際し、最近の作風の変化について語ってみたいと思います。

自分は当初、黒インクのみで単色の作品を描いていました。元来、線描への興味が強かったことに加え色彩に苦手意識があり、色を積極的に使うつもりはありませんでした。長年描いてゆくうちに白黒の画面に何か変化が欲しいなと思うようになりました。白黒の画面に少し青を加えるイメージで描いた作品が色を使用した最初です。現在使う色は青と赤・それに紫をたまに使います。ひとつの作品の中で、青なら青と規定したうえで色味の異なる青系のインクを複数使い分けています。

よく二項対立的な位置づけでとらわれがちな青と赤ですが、このふたつの色の性質は質的に大きく異なると常々感じています。私の作品の場合、青を使う場合には白黒の線描になんとなく青色を加えても大きく失敗はしません。青は明度的に黒に近いため、白黒の画面に加えてもうまくなじんでくれるからです。ですが同じように赤を使ってしまうと大抵赤色がぼやけた印象になります。細かくびっしりとした線描の隙間に赤を入れたところで赤色はなじんでくれず、赤特有の強さは表現できないのです。ぼやけた赤など赤ではありません・・。赤を効果的に使うことは本当に至難の業です。赤をどう使うかはまだまだ今後の課題です。赤は黒と対決させる意識で使っていかなければならないと今はなんとなく考えています。

色味の異なる複数の色を組み合わせることは現状考えていませんが、メインの青や赤に近い色を二種類・三種類と加えて色の幅を得ることは検討しています。

On the Subject of Color

With the publication of my second collection of works, I'd like to discuss the recent changes in my artistic style. Initially, I created monochromatic pieces using only black ink. Due to my strong affinity for line drawings and a certain hesitancy with regards to color, I had no intention of actively incorporating colors into my work. However, over the years, I began to desire a change in the black-and-white scene. The first step towards using colors in my work involved envisioning pieces where I added a touch of blue to the monochromatic screen. Currently, the colors I use include blue, red, and occasionally purple. Within a single piece, I deliberately choose a shade of blue and employ different ink colors within that spectrum.

Blue and red are often seen as binary opposites, but I've consistently felt that these two colors have significantly different qualities. In my work, when I introduce blue, it rarely leads to significant mistakes, even when I casually incorporate it into the black-and-white lines. This is because blue is close to black in terms of brightness and seamlessly integrates into the monochromatic picture. However, when I use red in a similar manner, it usually results in a blurry impression. Red fails to blend well within the fine, densely packed lines and doesn't capture the distinctive intensity of the color. A blurry red is not red at all... Effectively using red is indeed a formidable challenge. I currently have a vague notion that using red should involve a conscious confrontation with black, but this remains a task for the future. How to use red effectively is still a puzzle I need to solve.

At the moment, I haven't considered combining multiple colors with different hues. Nevertheless, I am contemplating the addition of a couple of colors close to my primary blue and red to expand my palette.

關於色彩

在第二本作品集的出版之際，我想談談最近我的藝術風格的變化。一開始，我只使用黑色墨水創作單色作品。由於我一直對線條畫風有濃厚的興趣，再加上對色彩有些不自信，所以並不打算積極運用顏色。然而，經過多年的繪畫過程，我開始渴望在黑白畫面中引入一些變化。我的第一幅使用色彩的作品是以在黑白畫面中加入一些藍色想法繪製而成。現在常使用的色彩有藍色、紅色，偶爾也會使用紫色。在同一幅作品中選擇藍色後，會使用不同色調的藍色墨水以增添變化。

藍色和紅色經常被以二元對立的方式看待，對於這兩種顏色的特性在質上有著顯著的不同常有體會。對於我的作品而言，當我使用藍色時，即使隨意地在黑白線條上加入藍色，也不容易出現大的失誤。因為藍色在亮度上接近黑色，因此即使加入黑白畫面中，也可以很好地融合。而紅色通常會呈現模糊的印象，即使在細小而密集的線條之間添加紅色，也無法融入反而凸顯紅色特有的強烈感。模糊的紅並不是紅色 ... 要有效地使用紅色實在是相當困難的事情。我現在有種模糊的概念，即使用紅色應該在某種程度上意識到將其與黑色對立，但這仍然是我未來的課題之一。如何運用紅色是一個需要深入思考的問題。

目前，我並未考慮結合多種不同色調的顏色，但我考慮選擇類似主要的藍色和紅色之類的顏色，再加上兩種或三種相近的色調，以擴展我的色彩範圍。

水彩表現について

2020 年頃から作風にさらに変化が欲しいと思い、ウェット・イン・ウェット（wet in wet）を作品に導入しました。ウェット・イン・ウェット（またはウェット・オン・ウェットともいう）は水彩技法のひとつで、水であらかじめ画面をしっかり湿らせ、乾かないうちに水で溶いた水彩絵の具やインクを落として画面上でにじみを作る技法です。この技法は「たらしこみ」という技法名で日本の伝統絵画、特に江戸期の琳派と呼ばれる作家たちの作品でもよく使われています。これは中国絵画における「破墨法」に近い技法です。
かっちりとした緻密な線描が身上である自分の作品には、水彩ならではのにじみを生かすこのウェット・イン・ウェットは真逆の技法のように思われるかもしれません。ですが自分としてはこの線描とにじみのコントラストを非常に気に入っています。堅い線描の、ともすれば息苦しい印象を観る人に与えそうな作風に程よい柔らかなアクセントを加えてくれていると思います。ウェット・イン・ウェットは水に水分の多い色を垂らす、半ば偶然性に支配された技法ではありますが、なるべく筆で水の色をコントロールするつもりで使っています。今後この技法が自分の中でアクセント以上の存在になるかどうか、作家本人にとっても楽しみなところです。

On Watercolor Expression

Around 2020, I sought further transformation in my artistic style and introduced the "wet-in-wet" technique into my works. "Wet-in-wet" is a watercolor technique which the paper is pre-moistened, and watercolor paint or ink are dropped onto the wet surface before it dries, creating a blurred effect. This technique, known as "tarashikomi" in traditional Japanese painting, was commonly used by artists of the Rinpa school during the Edo period and bears similarities to the "splashed ink" technique in Chinese painting.

For someone like me, known for precise and intricate line drawings, employing the "wet in wet" technique in watercolors to create a blurred effect may seem like a complete departure. However, I genuinely appreciate the contrast between the sharp lines and the blurriness. It adds a subtle softness to my otherwise rigid line-based style, offering a breath of fresh air to viewers. While "wet in wet" is a technique dominated by the semi-random nature of dropping water-rich colors into watercolor, I endeavor to control the color of water as much as possible with my brush. Whether this technique will become more than just an accent in my work is a matter of excitement and exploration for me in the future.

關於水彩表現

大約在 2020 年左右，我希望為我的藝術風格帶來更多變化，於是引入了 " 濕畫法 "（wet in wet）技法到我的作品中。" 濕畫法 " 是一種水彩技法，它通過在畫布事先充分濕潤的情況下，在畫布未乾的情況下使用水溶水彩顏料或墨水，以在畫布上產生模糊的效果。這種技法在日本的傳統繪畫中，特別是江戶時期的琳派畫家的作品中被廣泛使用，被稱為 " 滴灑 " 技法。這與中國畫中的 " 潑墨法 " 相似。對於一直以來以嚴謹的線條畫風為主的我來說，利用水彩的 " 濕畫法 " 技法來展現模糊的效果似乎截然不同。然而，我非常喜歡這種線條和模糊之間的對比。它為我的堅實線條畫風增添了柔和的亮點，可能會為觀眾帶來一些呼吸自由的感覺。雖然 " 濕畫法 " 是一種在水溶水彩中滴入水分較多的顏色，並且在某種程度上受到偶然性的支配的技法，但我儘量用筆來控制水的顏色。未來，這種技法是否會成為我作品中的一個重要元素，對於我本人來說也是一個令人期待的問題。

制作道具

ペンは専らロットリング社のイソグラフ（Rotring Isograph）を使用しています。最細の0.13mmで線を描いていましたが最近廃番になってしまったため、手持ちの0.13のスペアが終了次第、ステッドラーのマルスマチック（Staedtler Marsmatic）に切り替える予定です。なかなかローテク作家には厳しいご時世ですが、臨機応変にやっていこうと思っています。

主線はイソグラフ用の専用インクで描いています。黒はドクターマーチン（Dr.Ph.Martin's）のブラックスター、他にドクターマーチンの顔料系インクを使用しています。

インクのみですと淡い色が使えませんので顔料系マーカーも使用しています。

Creating Props

I exclusively use Rotring's Isograph pens for my work. I used to draw lines with the finest 0.13mm tip, but unfortunately, it has been discontinued recently. So, once I exhaust my remaining 0.13mm spare tips, I plan to switch to Staedtler's Marsmatic pens. It's a challenging time for low-tech artists like me, but I intend to adapt flexibly.
I draw the main lines using dedicated ink for Isograph pens. For black ink, I use Dr. Ph. Martin's "Black Star," and I also use other pigment-based inks from Dr. Ph. Martin.
Since ink alone doesn't allow for lighter colors, I also use pigment-based markers for my work.

德克特‧馬丁 (Dr. Ph. Martin's) 的彩色墨水

製作道具

我使用羅特靈 (Rotring) 公司生產的愛索格拉夫 (Isograph) 針筆。我一直使用最細的 0.13 毫米筆尖繪畫，但不幸地是最近這種筆款已經停產了。因此，一旦我手上的 0.13 毫米筆尖用盡，未來打算轉而使用施德樂 (Staedtler) 的馬爾斯瑪特 (Marsmatic) 筆。對於一位藝術家來說，現今世代對低科技的工具使用者來說確實存在一定的挑戰，但我打算靈活應對，繼續前進。

我使用專門為愛索格拉夫筆設計的墨水來繪製主要的線條。黑色墨水我使用的是德克特‧馬丁 (Dr. Ph. Martin's) 的「黑星」(Black Star) 色號，此外，我還使用了德克特‧馬丁的其他彩色墨水。

因為單純的墨水無法提供淺色效果，所以我還使用了顏料型的繪圖筆來進行繪畫。

德國羅特靈 (rOtring) 生產的 Isograph 針筆

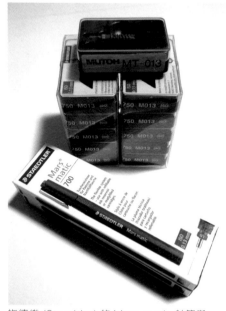

施德樂 (Staedtler) 的 Mars matic 針筆與 0.13mm 筆尖

制作の手順

パネルに水張りしたケント紙に 5B くらいの鉛筆で軽く下絵を描いていきます。別の紙にドローイングを描くことはしません。鉛筆で下絵を描きながら形や構図を決めていきます。

構図がある程度決まったらペンで描いていきます。模様はその都度描いていますが、これまでの制作である程度パターン化されています。粗密のバランスを考えつつ描きます。

色も線と同時進行で入れます。白と黒・濃い色と薄い色のバランスを考えながら描いています。

地道な描画作業の繰り返しです。

The Production Process

I start by lightly sketching the outline with a 5B pencil on Kent paper that has been stretched on a panel. I usually do not draw the artwork draft on a separate sheet of paper. While sketching with the pencil, I determine the shapes and composition.

Once the composition is somewhat established, I proceed to ink it using a pen. While the patterns are drawn on an ad hoc basis, they have become somewhat standardized through previous work. I carefully consider the balance between detail and boldness as I draw.

Colors are introduced concurrently with the lines. I contemplate the balance between light and dark, as well as between white and black, while drawing.

It's a repetitive process of diligent drawing work.

以鉛筆輕輕勾勒輪廓

創作過程

首先我將日本肯特紙輕輕固定在畫板上，再使用 5B 鉛筆輕輕勾勒輪廓線條。我通常不會在另一張紙上繪製草圖，而是直接在這張已經裱好的肯特紙上創作。使用鉛筆繪製的同時逐漸確定創作形狀和構圖。

一旦構圖在某種程度上確定下來，接下來使用針筆進行描繪。儘管圖案是根據即興想法繪製的，但在以往的作品中圖案樣式已經變得有些標準化。在繪畫過程中會仔細考慮細節和粗糙之間的平衡，力求呈現出完美的效果。

顏色部分是與輪廓線條同步進行的，我在繪畫過程中會深思熟慮黑與白、深與淺之間的平衡，確保整體畫面的協調性。

這是一個重複且需要細心的創作過程，同時需要不斷地進行細緻的工作。

再以針筆進行繪製

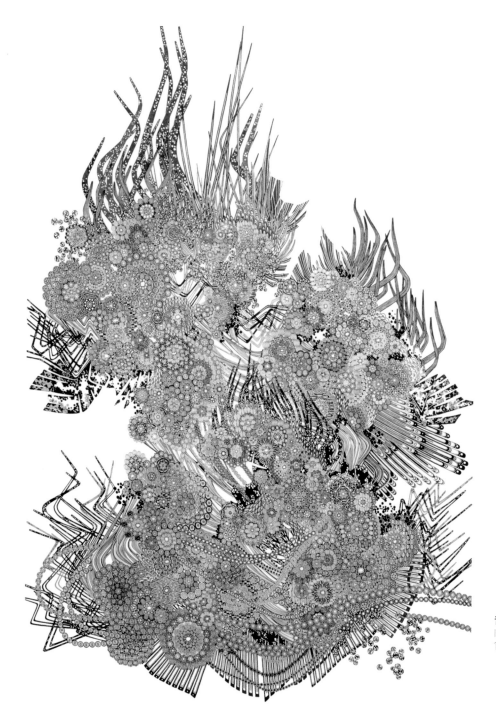

青盛 (Seisei), 2017
Ink on Kent Paper
116.7 × 80.3 (cm)

青縞 (Aotoki), 2018
Ink on Kent Paper
Φ 22.7(cm)

緋掌 (Hisho), 2018
Ink on Kent Paper
Φ 22.7(cm)

緋斂 (Hiren), 2018
Ink on Kent Paper
Φ 22.7(cm)

紫閑 (Shikan), 2018
Ink on Kent Paper
72.2 × 60.6 (cm)

激緋 (Gekihi), 2018
Ink on Kent Paper
53.0 × 33.3(cm)

紫蓉 (Shiyo), 2018
Ink on Kent Paper
22.7 × 15.8(cm)

紫鶉 (Shikun), 2018
Ink on Kent Paper
41.0 × 31.8(cm)

青奭 (Seiso), 2019
Ink on Kent Paper
18.0 × 18.0(cm)

紫殺(Shikai), 2019
Ink on Kent Paper
22.7 × 15.8(cm)

紫羗 (Shiyu), 2019
Ink on Kent Paper
Φ 22.7(cm)

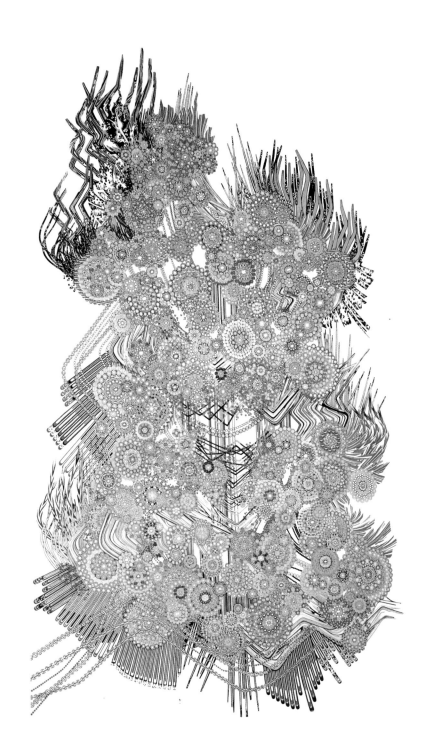

熾盛 (Shijo), 2019
ink on Kent paper
194.0 × 112.0(cm)

青冲 (Seityu), 2020
Ink on Kent Paper
22.7 × 15.8(cm)

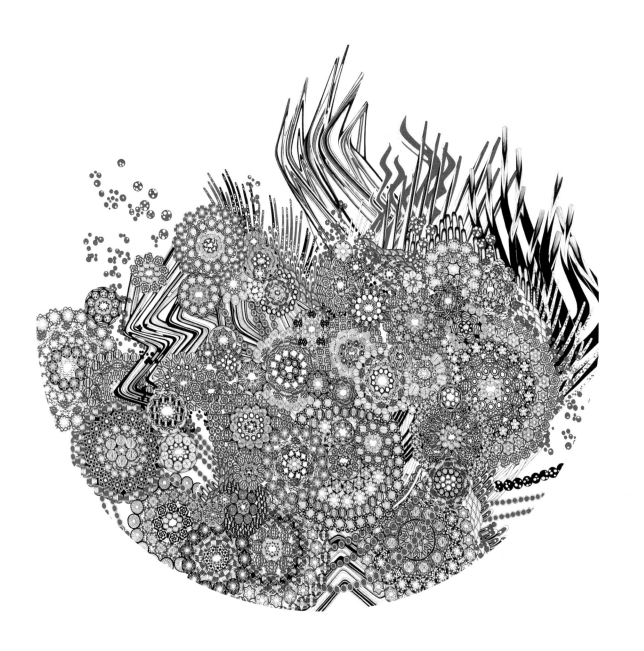

赫華 (Kakuka), 2020
ink on Kent paper
Φ 53.0(cm)

赫丸 (Kakumaru), 2020
ink on Kent paper
Φ 53.0(cm)

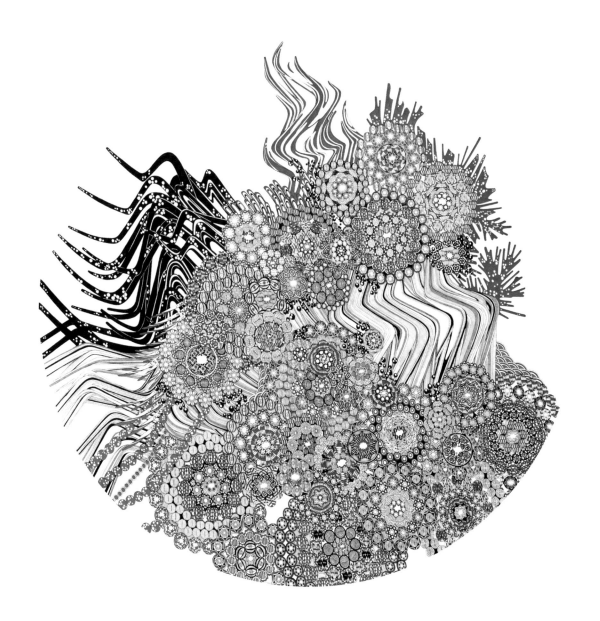

赫鵑 (Kakuken), 2020
ink on Kent paper
Φ 53.0(cm)

紅眩 (Kogen), 2020
ink on Kent paper
22.7 × 15.8(cm)

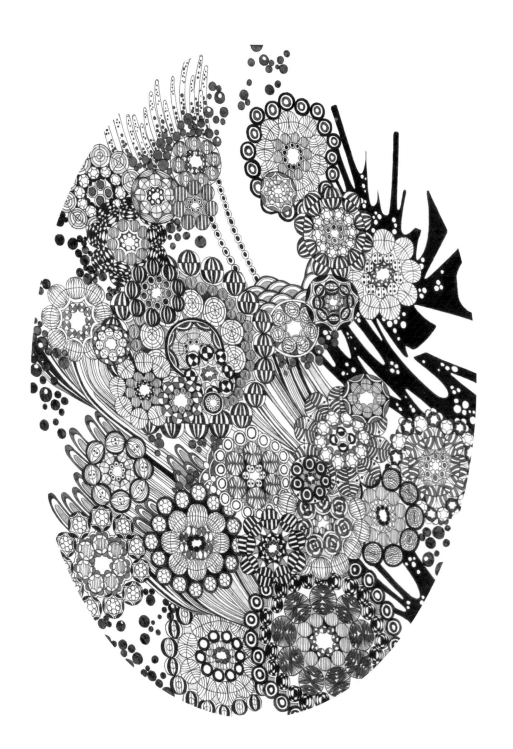

青彧 (Seilku), 2020
Ink on Kent Paper
Φ 22.7 × 15.8 (cm)

朱鷺 (Shurei), 2020
Ink on Kent Paper
41.0 × 31.8(cm)

紅爛 (Koran), 2020
Ink on Kent Paper
Φ 22.7(cm)

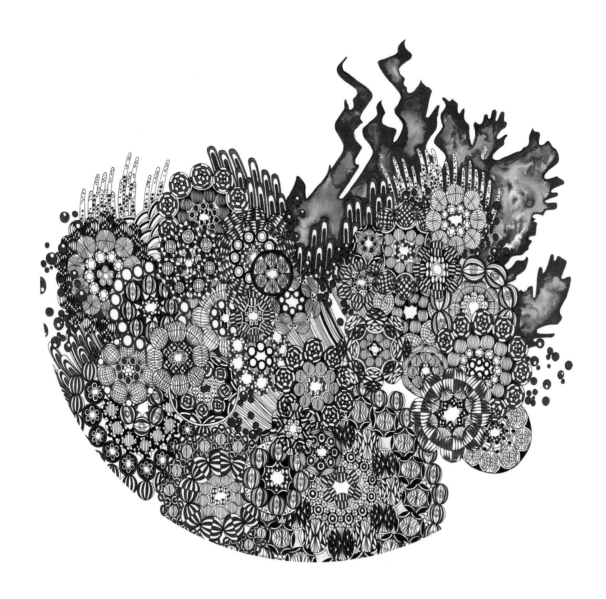

紅燐 (Korin), 2020
Ink on Kent Paper
Φ 22.7(cm)

紅盞 (Koto), 2020
Ink on Kent Paper
Φ 22.7(cm)

焱 (Yan), 2020
Ink on Kent Paper
33.3 × 21.0(cm)

黝 (Aoguro), 2021
ink on Kent paper
Φ 22.7 × 15.8(cm)

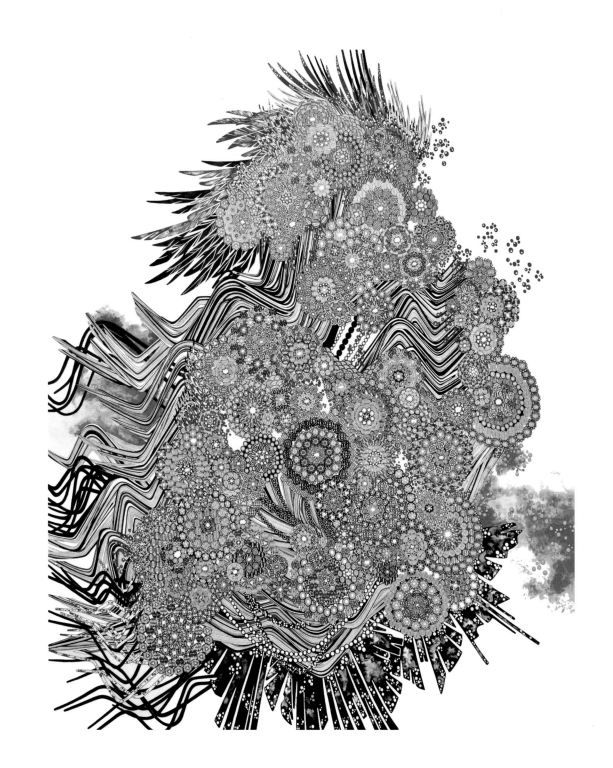

紅廖 (Koboku), 2021
ink on Kent paper
91.0 × 72.7(cm)

靉聲 (Shosei) , 2021
Ink on Kent Paper
Φ 22.7(cm)

靛鶄（Dianqing）, 2021
Ink on Kent Paper
Φ 80.0(cm)

青(Sei), 2021
Ink on Kent Paper
Φ 22.7(cm)

辰鳥（Shin）, 2021
ellipse ink on Kent paper
22.7 × 15.8(cm)

洲 (Suhama), 2021
Ink on Kent Paper
Φ 22.7 × 15.8 (cm)

青佩 (Seifu), 2021
Ink on Kent Paper
33.3 × 24.2 (cm)

泫澐 (Kenyun), 2021
Ink on Kent Paper
42.0 × 29.7(cm)

濴濴 (eiei), 2021
Ink on Kent Paper
Φ 53.0(cm)

青瀾 (Seiran), 2022
Ink on Kent Paper
Φ 53.0 (cm)

青洴 (Seisei), 2022
Ink on Kent Paper
33.3 × 22.0 (cm)

混彤 (Konton), 2022
ink on Kent paper
Φ 53.0(cm)

少耜 (Shokyoku), 2022
ink on Kent paper
22.7 × 15.8(cm)

莊莊 (Koukou), 2022
Ink on Kent Paper
33.3 × 24.2(cm)

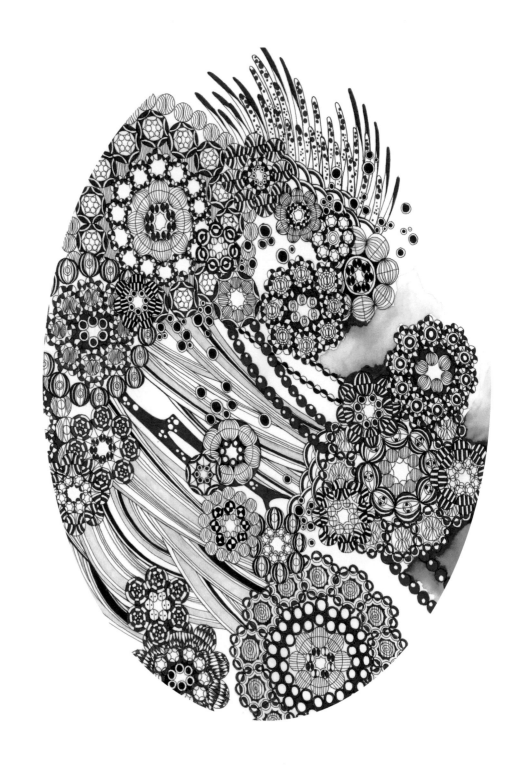

朱玎 (Syutei), 2023
ink on Kent paper
Φ 22.7 × 15.8(cm)

玉纏 (Gyokuzen), 2023
ink on Kent paper
Φ 22.7(cm)

List of works

2017

青盛 (Seisei), 2017
Ink on Kent Paper
116.7×80.3 (cm)

P.20

2018

青鵠 (Aotoki), 2018
Ink on Kent Paper
Φ22.7(cm)

P.21

緋掌 (Hisho), 2018
Ink on Kent Paper
Φ22.7(cm)

P.22

緋斂 (Hiren), 2018
Ink on Kent Paper
Φ22.7(cm)

P.23

紫闌 (Shikan), 2018
Ink on Kent Paper
72.2 × 60.6 (cm)

P.24

鬩緋 (Gekihi), 2018
Ink on Kent Paper
53.0×33.3(cm)

P.25

紫蓉 (Shiyo), 2018
Ink on Kent Paper
22.7×15.8(cm)

P.26

紫鶉 (Shikun), 2018
Ink on Kent Paper
41.0×31.8(cm)

P.27

2019

青奭 (Seiso), 2019
Ink on Kent Paper
18.0 × 18.0(cm)

P.28

紫殳(Shikai), 2019
Ink on Kent Paper
22.7 × 15.8(cm)

P.29

紫羑 (Shiyu), 2019
Ink on Kent Paper
Φ 22.7(cm)

P.30

熾盛 (Shijo), 2019
ink on Kent paper
194.0 × 112.0(cm)

P.31

2020

青冲 (Seityu), 2020
Ink on Kent Paper
22.7 × 15.8(cm)

P.32

赫華 (Kakuka), 2020
ink on Kent paper
Φ 53.0(cm)

P.33

赫丸 (Kakumaru), 2020
ink on Kent paper
Φ 53.0(cm)

P.34

赫鵑 (Kakuken), 2020
ink on Kent paper
Φ 53.0(cm)

P.35

紅眩 (Kogen), 2020
ink on Kent paper
22.7 × 15.8(cm)

P.36

青彧 (Seilku), 2020
Ink on Kent Paper
Φ 22.7 × 15.8 (cm)

P.37

朱鴒 (Shurei), 2020
Ink on Kent Paper
41.0 × 31.8(cm)

P.38

紅爛 (Koran), 2020
Ink on Kent Paper
Φ 22.7(cm)

P.39

2021

紅粼 (Korin), 2020
Ink on Kent Paper
Φ 22.7(cm)

P.40

紅盪 (Koto), 2020
Ink on Kent Paper
Φ 22.7(cm)

P.41

焱 (Yan), 2020
Ink on Kent Paper
33.3 × 21.0(cm)

P.42

黝 (Aoguro), 2021
ink on Kent paper
Φ 22.7 × 15.8(cm)

P.43